The Berenstain Bears
GET IN A FIGHT

When two small bears
Don't get along,
The grownups worry—
What went wrong?

A FIRST TIME BOOK®

The Berenstain Bears
GET IN A FIGHT

Stan & Jan Berenstain

Random House 🏠 New York

Copyright © 1982 by Berenstain Enterprises, Inc. All rights reserved. Published in the United States by Random House Children's Books, a division of Random House, Inc., New York. Random House and the colophon are registered trademarks of Random House, Inc. First Time Books and the colophon are registered trademarks of Berenstain Enterprises, Inc.
randomhouse.com/kids   BerenstainBears.com
Library of Congress Cataloging-in-Publication Data
Berenstain, Stan. The Berenstain bears get in a fight. (Berenstain bears first time books)
Summary: After causing a family commotion when they fight with each other, the Berenstain cubs learn that sometimes even the best of friends don't get along.
ISBN 978-0-394-85132-7 (trade)
[1. Behavior—Fiction. 2. Bears—Fiction. 3. Brothers and sisters—Fiction. 4. Friendship—Fiction.]
I. Berenstain, Jan. II. Title. III. Series: Berenstain, Stan. Berenstain bears first time books.
PZ7.B4483Beo   [E]   81-15866
Printed in the United States of America   90 89 88 87 86 85 84 83 82 81 80 79 78 77 76 75 74 73

Most mornings, in Bear Country, the sun
rose to greet the day and the mockingbird
sang its copycat songs outside an upstairs
window of the bears' tree house.

And inside the tree house Brother
Bear and Sister Bear would wake up.

Brother and Sister usually got along very well.

They took turns nicely with the bathroom.

They said "please" and "thank you" at breakfast.

They often sat together on the school bus.

And after school they worked together happily on their special project—their own backyard tree house.

But one gray morning Brother and Sister didn't get along well at all! Maybe it was the weather—or maybe it was because the mockingbird slept late. But whatever it was, Brother and Sister Bear got into a big fight. . . .

Sister Bear opened her eyes and stretched. Then she sat up and let her legs dangle over the edge of her bed—right in Brother Bear's face. She didn't do it to be rude. It was just one of those things that happens with bunk beds.

But that morning Brother was not in a very good mood.

"Sister!" he shouted. "Get your dopey feet out of my face!"

"My feet aren't dopey, and they're not
in your face!" she shouted back.
"Get your dopey *face* out of my face!"
snarled Brother.

"You shut up!" snapped Sister . . .

and before Brother could answer,
she skipped into the
bathroom ahead of him.

She took a *very long time* . . .

brushing her teeth,

washing up,

and brushing her fur.

"You'd better come out of that bathroom!" shouted Brother, banging on the door.

"Brother Bear," said Papa, coming out of his bedroom, "you know better than to shout at your sister." "But she's taking too long in the bathroom," complained Brother, "and she's doing it on purpose!"

When Brother raised his fist
to bang on the door again, it opened
and out came Sister, all spruced up.
"Good morning, Papa,"
she said, as nice
as you please.
"Gr-r-r!"
said Brother.

Brother and Sister didn't say "please" and "thank you" that morning at breakfast— because they weren't speaking to each other.

And they didn't sit together on the school bus. Sister sat in the front and Brother sat way in the back.

That afternoon they made a line down the middle of their backyard tree house to show which half was whose. It wasn't much fun sitting up there in their tree house not speaking.

Especially when it began to rain—hard!

Later they kept on being mean by taking back the things they usually shared.

Sister took back her modeling clay—which Brother had made into dinosaurs—and rolled it into one big lump.

Brother took back his trucks and planes and put them on the top shelf where Sister couldn't reach them.

They got so angry that they forgot they weren't speaking and began shouting at each other even louder than before. Then Papa lost his temper and began shouting at them to stop shouting.

The neighbors didn't know which was worse—the big storm or the racket coming from the bears' house.

Mama had quite enough. She put two fingers to her mouth and whistled—*very very loudly*. Papa and the cubs were so surprised that they stopped shouting.

"I didn't know you could whistle like that, Mama," said Sister.

"Well, I can. And I can also tell you," said Mama sternly, "that I've had quite enough of this foolish fighting. Why, I doubt you two even remember what you're fighting about!"

The cubs tried to remember, but they couldn't.

Mama took the cubs into her lap.
"Everybody gets into an argument
once in a while," she said. "Even
folks who love each
other very much."

"You and I don't have arguments,"
said Papa.

"Oh, yes, we do," said Mama.

"No, we don't," argued Papa.

"We're having one right now," said
Mama, "about whether or not we have
arguments!"

While Papa thought that one over, Mama went on to say that occasional arguments are part of living together.

"We get angry, even call each other names and say things we really don't mean—and after a while it's over."

"Like the storm?" asked Sister. The rain had almost stopped, and the sun was beginning to shine through the clouds.

"Yes," said Mama. "Like the storm."
"Look!" said Papa.

The sun shining on the last of
the rain had made a rainbow.

"A rainbow is something very beautiful that happens after a storm," said Mama, looking at the cubs.

"You mean like making up after a big fight?"

"Sort of," said Mama.

So Brother and Sister Bear
hugged and made up.
    And got along just beautifully—
until the next time, anyway.